"*Expedition* sits in an unexpected and thrilling overlap between do-we-have-our-first-52-year-old-woman-*Bourne-Identity*-style-thriller or is this a woman on the verge of unleashing curious psychic potential, and a lovely meditation on loneliness. Vogrin entertains readers with Margo Webster's thoughtful and clear voice while giving them the space to consider their own relationships to reality."

—Megan Giddings, *Lakewood and The Women Could Fly*

"This suspenseful novella is alternately eerie and funny, enigmatic and specific. Valerie Vogrin's exploration of what happens when a previous life is demolished is also a mesmerizing cataloging of what we rebuild with, from fragile trust to pizza rolls. I didn't want to stop reading."

—Caitlin Horrocks, *The Vexations* and *Life Among the Terranauts*

"Reader, prepare yourself to meet Margo, a woman either at wit's end or on the verge of transcendence, or possibly both. In Valerie Vogrin's propulsive and often hilarious novella, *Expedition*, we are taken for a short spin by a narrator who hasn't quite gotten it all figured out yet, but whose fears, doubts, and anxieties nonetheless feel like our own. I devoured this in a single sitting, grateful, sated."

—Anthony Varallo, *What Did You Do Today?*

"Valerie Vogrin's *Expedition* is a taut, unsettling novella about the meaning of self. What starts as a mystery rife with paranoia becomes a study of discovery, then blossoms into a story about the strength and affirmation of female friendships. *Expedition* stays with you like the remnants of a disquieting dream."

—Jamey Bradbury, *The Wild Inside*

"On their *Expedition*, Valerie Vogrin and her hero, Margo Webster, explore not only the wonders of the world, but the wonders of memory and identity, transforming Margo into someone she never knew and someone she never would have been. The journey is a life-altering ride for Margo, one I couldn't wait to unfold, fighting to get to the next page, consuming it all in one satisfying sitting."

—Michael Czyzniejewski, *The Amnesiac in the Maze: Stories*

"I've been waiting a long time for a new Valerie Vogrin book, and *Expedition* is even weirder and smarter and more beautiful than I had dared hope."

—Kyle Minor, *Praying Drunk*

Expedition

—

Valerie Vogrin

UNIVERSITY OF TAMPA PRESS

POMME

Manufactured in the United States of America
First Edition

On the Cover: *Entry Request*, Sophia Lavallee, 2023, digital photograph.

Cover design by Jay Aja

The University of Tampa Press
401 West Kennedy Boulevard
Tampa, FL 33606

ISBN 978-1-59732-226-3 (pbk.)
ISBN 978-1-59732-227-0 (hbk.)
ISBN 978-1-59732-228-7 (ebook)

Library of Congress Control Number:
2025943098

Browse & order online at
http://utpress.ut.edu

Expedition

for Kevin

Mine is the old story of starting over. If there is something that makes my story special, it's my extreme lack of self-knowledge—a lack that isn't exactly or entirely my own fault.

Let me explain.

I was a just-hired employee of a small, government-sponsored humanitarian organization, and a new arrival in Africa. I'd been waiting several days for news of the bus that would transport me to my assigned village when I was bitten by a snake. My hand blazed with pain and immediately began to swell. My host family reacted with efficient panic. They cleaned the wound, kept my hand elevated, and borrowed a Jeep to rush me to the nearest clinic where organization doctors administered an experimental synthetic antivenom. The antivenom worked brilliantly and I was released after a one-night stay. But about a week later—still having received no update on the bus—I began to experience an array of troubling symptoms—blurred vision, high fever, intermittent partial paralysis, difficulty swallowing, a heightened sense of smell, hallucinations. Sometimes the walls seemed to tremble and sometimes I saw fabulous things.

The moths appeared at dusk—a pair of enormous cobalt-blue moths resting on the rough walls of my hut.

Those moths: undulating, dusty, black-daubed wings, each marked with a gold, glowing eyespot. Their six-foot wingspan. The flicker of their feathery antennae. The aroma of damp coffee grounds and the air humming like an electric field. I wanted nothing more than to reach out and touch a wing, but I couldn't move my arms.

What followed was like a childhood illness—a period of being talked over and fussed with and groggy, achy helplessness. I remember a lot of blood draws and unidentified fluids administered intravenously.

I was released after a clinic stay of who-knows-how-long. The fever was gone, and the organization's medical staff said my blood work was normal and my organs and various systems were in shipshape order. The staff explained that I'd suffered from a severe viral infection. There was, they emphasized, no connection between the antivenom and my illness.

I vaguely recall a debriefing of sorts. A sense of menace pervaded the dingy room. There may or may not have been a black-and-yellow lizard edging up the cinder block wall. I remember signing documents—I'm guessing a liability waiver and a nondisclosure agreement—and a stern voice speaking of consequences. Someone thanked me for my service, and someone handed me a lukewarm bottle of Coke.

⸻

My first memory of being back in the U.S. is pulling my carry-on suitcase through Terminal 5 of O'Hare. I was woozy and my tongue felt swollen. The terminal reeked of cinnamon and french fries. A red plastic wallet held my driver's license, $500 in cash, and a U.S. Bank debit card. On the back was a sticky note bearing a four-digit number I assumed was the PIN. I recognized my cell phone—it had a faded Save the Whales decal on the back. But the phone had been wiped—no record of calls or texts, no internet history. There were only two numbers under Contacts. One was labeled Mom&Dad. The one labeled Home had the local area code—312.

I sat at an empty gate and opened my suitcase. I sorted the items into piles, one for the things I didn't recognize at all and another for things I sensed were mine: white cotton panties, a brown linen skirt, an embroidered peasant blouse, several cotton T-shirts in different shades of blue, and a pair of jeans.

My name, Margo Webster; my age, fifty-two; my phone; and the simple fabric of the clothing—at that moment this was all I knew about myself. The crooks of both my arms held fading bruises. Two small, round scars marked the top of my left hand.

I sat there for a while longer until the gate began to fill for a flight to Lisbon. I ate a raspberry yogurt and drank two bottles of water. I felt both eagerness and anxiety before calling the Home number. The North Carolina driver's license, issued three years before in 2006, showed an address in Durham. Had I moved to Chicago? Was anyone anywhere expecting me?

The woman who answered, Deborah, was confused by my confusion, and wary. She officiously explained that I had booked and prepaid a three-month stay at the studio apartment above her garage in Evanston. There were no refunds, did I understand that? Once I assured her that I did, she relaxed a bit. She recited the address very slowly as if sensing my infirmity.

—

I slept. I walked the neighborhood. The apartment was a few blocks from Northwestern, less than a mile from the beach—a place I was drawn to. The names of the shops and restaurants meant nothing to me. It didn't seem possible that I had made these living arrangements for myself.

I visited the public library almost every day. I worked on the library computers, making sure to delete my search history before logging off. I read for hours, hiding my books-in-progress on seldom-visited shelves.

I compared the scars on my hand to photos I found on the web. My scars were similar to the marks left by venomous snakes, but they could have resulted from spider bites or insect stings.

Many of my original complaints had disappeared or abated, except it appeared I was experiencing retrograde amnesia, although as far as I knew, I hadn't suffered a traumatic brain injury, severe trauma, or repeated concussions—the typical causes listed for the condition.

—

My most vivid memory was the smell of my grandparents' basement in Milwaukee—bleach and Tide and flowery fabric softener and mildew. I remembered riding a blue tricycle as far as I dared into the dim empty corners while Grandma did laundry. I remembered walking to the grocery store with Grandpa and the yellow wagon we took turns pulling.

I remembered that I lived with them because my parents were in Peru doing missionary work. From bits of overheard conversations, I learned that my parents hadn't intended to have children. They owed fealty to God alone. My mother gave me a Bible each May when they visited for two weeks. My mother told me that God had a plan for me and cried when I told her I didn't pray. During one visit she hectored me until I'd memorized John 1:1–5. *In the beginning was the Word.* Her bushy black eyebrows swooped and plummeted as she read scripture. My father had a bristly red mustache and kept his distance.

On the weekends, Grandma, Grandpa, and I sometimes went to Veterans' Park or McKinley Park. We beachcombed and flew kites, and I learned to swim. Grandpa smelled like cigarettes and Ivory soap. He collected postage stamps. Grandma wore Cashmere Bouquet Talcum Powder. She kept twenty-dollar bills rolled up inside the body of a battery-less flashlight beneath the bathroom sink.

I recalled details about my grade school classrooms and teachers. I remember my lips aching when I began playing the trumpet and the fierce burn of strep throat when I was ten.

I knew the name of my high school and college and the university I attended for graduate school, but I had very few clear memories after about the age of eleven. There was only absence— an echoey, empty closet—where my life should have been.

I knew I had studied public health and environmental science and taught for some time. I believed I had gone to Africa to work on a water safety project focused on establishing piped water connections. I could summon up facts and procedures related to water contamination and chlorination and waterborne diseases like typhoid fever and cholera, and the statistics were horrifying, but the knowledge didn't feel connected to me. I knew that my grandparents were dead and that my parents remained in South America. I had no reason to think we had grown closer. Whoever I had been, I no longer was.

I began assembling a self from the things I'd enjoyed as a kid—British mysteries I'd read with Grandma, picking up intriguing stones on a Lake Michigan beach, and eating chocolate chip cookie dough ice cream, cinnamon toast, and apple slices dipped in peanut butter. My favorite color was blue. I sat cross-legged. I liked cats and marching bands.

It was hard to think of myself as an adult.

My symptoms were invisible. There's no way to prove the existence of a hallucination or the difficulty of distinguishing reality from nonreality.

I didn't possess any correspondence or paperwork from the organization.

When, after a week of bureaucratic runaround, I reached someone who admitted to having access to my employment records, I was told I'd completed a two-week cultural training intensive in Washington, DC, but subsequently failed a drug test and was let go. When I insisted that I'd been to Africa, the employee explained that the organization hadn't sent any new teams overseas in the past eight months. I began to cry in frustration and the employee's voice softened. "Are you all right, honey?" she drawled.

I had no memory of myself as a drug user. My instinct said this was laughable. I knew I had been to Africa. (And part of me knew it was possible that I hadn't.)

Without my passport, I had no evidence of my travel—few clues at all regarding what had happened to me. Working at the library computers, I tried a variety of search terms in different combinations—the name of the organization, Africa, snake bites, antivenom, side effects, hallucinations, etc. I found nothing linking the organization to antivenom side effects. I did find reports of serum sickness in individuals who were treated with *non*-synthetic antivenom. Their symptoms were those of a bad allergy reaction—no psychosis, no hallucinations—and they subsided within a few days. I could understand the organization denying that I'd been ill, but why deny I had traveled to Africa under their auspices?

Once I received a copy of my birth certificate, I could apply for a replacement passport, but that would prove nothing because it turned out that there is no government agency that tracks travel history (at least no agency known to Google). I could submit an information request to U.S. Customs and Border Protection, although online commenters complained that it involved a lot of paperwork and no guarantee of success. If I had traveled under a visa, the embassy of the country I'd visited would have a record of me, but I couldn't remember the name of the country. I recited the names of the eight African nations in which the organization had projects, but they were as flat in my mouth as spelling bee words.

The U.S. Bank account held $10,000. I didn't remember how or why I'd received it. Was this redress? Wages? A bribe? Drug money? Its unknown origin wasn't the kind of problem that not having money would have been, but the money didn't feel like something I could count on.

I couldn't shake the feeling of unseen hands directing my life, and each time I thought this, I pictured my mother's eyebrows lifting in triumph.

So—what next? Would my symptoms abate or worsen? Would my memory improve? Would someone from the organization contact me? Were they monitoring my actions? Was there a better option than wait and see? (I couldn't think of one.) Some days the three-month term of my rental agreement felt like a promise and other days it felt like a threat.

I met Loren at Sharkey's, a dive bar near Deborah's house, a few weeks after arriving in Chicago. I had started going there midafternoon before it began filling with students and other locals. I found the click of pool balls pleasing. I had an inkling that I might know how to play.

Loren told me he was thirty years old, a part-time waiter, and aspiring stand-up comic.

"I have severe tree nut allergies. I'm a not-bad ukulele player and my favorite color is yellow." This last bit partly explained his eye-poppingly bright Hawaiian print shirt.

"Good to know," I said. His shirt and straightforward manner and shaggy blonde hair amused me. "I'll keep my peanuts and cashews to myself."

"I'm grateful," he said, laughing. "So, what's your story?"

"I haven't had nearly enough beers to say."

"C'mon, give me something to work with." He flashed a wicked set of dimples.

"I'm unemployed, and I played trumpet when I was a kid."

"That's not much to go on," he said. "Are you intentionally unemployed or . . ." He took a hasty drink of his beer. "Sorry—I get it if you don't want to talk about it."

I told him I'd recently been very sick and that my brain wasn't working properly. "I'm recuperating," I said.

"Me too," he said. He was recovering from a bad break up that left him sleeping on the couch of various friends. He'd had a run of mediocre auditions. His sense of timing was off. He felt sleepy most of the time. "I'm sorry," he said, eventually. "Me, me, me."

"Don't worry about it," I said.

"So, what's wrong with your brain?" He smacked his palm against his forehead. "Gah! There I go again."

I took a long draw on my beer. I could blow off his question or I could not. It felt like a turning point.

He fiddled with a beer mat, giving me time to make up my mind—another point in his favor.

"I have amnesia, and sometimes I have a hard time knowing what's real." It didn't feel as bad as I thought it would to say this out loud.

"Amnesia—is that really a thing?" he asked.

"What do you mean?"

"I thought that was something that only happened to people on TV and in movies."

"Um . . . I'm pretty sure amnesia falls under the category of common knowledge."

He flushed. "There's a lot of them. *50 First Dates, The Bourne Identity* . . . Though now that I think of it, it makes sense that they're based on something real. Sorry. I guess my brain isn't working properly either."

"It's okay."

"*Finding Nemo, Memento* . . ."

"Really. You can let it go."

He studied my face. "You don't know those movies, do you?"

I shook my head. "The last movie I remember seeing is *Jungle Book*."

"That really sucks. Is it permanent—your condition? I mean, what do the doctors say?"

"Give it some time." At least that was the consensus of the online medical experts. My glass was empty. "Do you want another beer?"

"I'll get this round," he said.

"You got the last one."

"But . . . I mean, I have a job."

"I'm fine for money," I said. "I don't need a job at the moment."

"Interesting," he said.

"I'm thinking maybe I'll go back to school," I quickly added.

"Sometimes I think that, too," he said. "Anyway, you can get the next round." He headed to the bar with our empty glasses.

I could see that it might be good to have someone to talk to. I hadn't known I was considering school until it came up in conversation. I was glad to discover I had a sense of humor.

—

Loren was grateful for a place to sleep that wasn't a lumpy couch. I appreciated having someone to help me gauge reality. *Is that guy in the corner booth watching me? Wasn't that white car parked across the street yesterday, too? Does my face look okay?* Loren was very patient with his responses. *I think that guy is*

*actually asleep. That was an Audi, this is a Subaru. Your face is fine
and dandy.*

He did observational humor about customer service jobs and
living in the city. His jokes were unremarkable, yet I found them
genuinely funny. We both had low libidos—mine by nature (I
guessed) and his thanks to antidepressant side effects—and we
appeared to share an utter lack of shame regarding what some
people might think of as wasting colossal amounts of time. We fit
into each other's schedules. He worked the breakfast and brunch
shift while I went to the library. Afternoons, we met to play pool
and watch baseball at Sharkey's. My bank shot needed work, but I
had a powerful break and good aim and usually won. Back at the
apartment, we binge-watched cooking show competitions and ate
microwaved meals. Deborah was a low-key landlord. She didn't
object when I told her that Loren would be staying with me, and
only sometimes did I smell gasoline when she left her car running
for too long in the garage before pulling out.

Some days I still used the library's computers to look for
information related to what happened to me. I studied photos
and updates of the organization's work in Africa. Plenty of
work had taken place in the past year, and although I found no
proof that the woman on the phone had lied to me, there was
no indication that this work involved newly arrived staff. (One
of the organization's goals was to train and empower locals as
employees and volunteers.) Some of the photos looked familiar:
a woman in a red shirt and bandana smiling as she filled a glass
from a reinforced pipe; power lines running above clusters of
huts with thatched roofs. But I might have encountered scenes
like this in a movie.

I began to spend more time reading mysteries than researching, and my googling became less methodical. I entered search terms plucked from my memory, bits of remembered facts and events, as well as topics I'd been avoiding, like my parents. Their mission's website referenced verifiable statistics on Peruvian demographics; however, I questioned the reliability of its depiction of the mission's work with the Asháninka people. The text boasted of assisting local ministries in "planting" churches in this region of the Amazon rainforest. (There were a lot of gardening metaphors.) They claimed that as the people abandoned their old shamanistic beliefs and barbaric rituals and grew in God's Word, they were liberated from the fear of evil spirits. I clicked on the "Who We Are" button. There they were at the top of the list: the elderly version of my parents, tall and grizzled, faces deeply tanned and gaunt and pious. My father had grown a thick gray beard with no trace of red in it. My mother's faded green shift had an uneven, self-righteous hem. It was almost funny that whoever wiped my cell phone kept their number in the contact list.

Some days I did little more than check the weather forecast before heading to my favorite chair to read—I was working my way through the Hercule Poirot series.

—

We were into our second month of this routine when Loren looked up from a bowl of popcorn and said, "I've decided to head back home for a while and regroup. An old friend of mine at the Comedy Barn can guarantee me a couple of slots a week."

"That makes sense." I had anticipated something like this. I knew Loren was frustrated by his inability to break into the

Chicago comedy scene, and he hated waiting tables. This city wasn't ideal for a thin-skinned, gentle-humored guy like Loren.

"I was thinking . . ." he continued, "Why don't you come, too?"

I coughed out a laugh.

"I mean it," he said.

Huh. I tried to gather my thoughts. I only had a few weeks left on my agreement with Deborah, but she'd told me I was welcome to renew.

"Move in with your family? I don't think so." This sounded like a normal response.

"Not *with* them," Loren clarified. "There's a whole separate apartment with a private entrance. Mom was planning to rent it out."

"In southern Illinois? I'm not really equipped for country life." I still couldn't take him seriously.

"C'mon. It'll give you a chance to check out the university, college town life—see if it suits you."

Loren had said only positive things about his kid sister and his mother, Audrey. His sister, Erica, was sixteen. She was involved in a lot of extracurricular activities. His mom was a nurse and had started taking night classes. She'd been through a hard time, but she was doing better. His grandmother was a hoot. That wasn't much to go on, but there were no obvious red flags, either. Of course, I had to wonder what the hell they would make of unhinged, unrooted, fifty-two-year-old me.

Loren was sitting on the couch. The day's gaudy shirt was a jumble of serrated leaves and owls. He'd set the empty popcorn bowl beside him. In that moment, I couldn't recall how we'd met at

Sharkey's. He'd been sitting at the bar reading a book (what book?) and I'd asked him about it? Maybe. Or had he approached me and initiated conversation?

What did it matter? We'd started talking. We clicked. Things like that happened every day. He almost certainly hadn't been sent by the organization to keep an eye on me.

What I was sure of: My days were less empty with Loren around. I felt safer, too. This was in the second year of the Obama administration, and despite all my various problems, I wasn't immune to a sense of optimism, to the shiny promise of a new place. Leaving Chicago was almost certainly my decision, and I liked the feel of that.

A 1970s rec room had been reconstituted in the walkout basement apartment, including a two-toned orange shag carpet, a glass-topped coffee table, and an orange-and-brown plaid sofa bed with matching side chairs. Bullfight posters hung behind a chrome bar and barstools. The minifridge was stocked with orange juice and Corona, and the tiny freezer compartment was stuffed with pizza rolls and other frozen snacks we heated in the toaster oven. We fell back into watching cooking shows. We napped a lot.

Occasionally, Loren stepped into the backyard to talk on the phone. On day three, he left to meet his friend at the comedy club. Only in these brief interludes of solitude was I really aware of his family's comings and goings overhead—footsteps, cupboard doors banging shut, the shuddering vibration of a washing machine. At mealtimes, I saw movement beneath the door at the top of the basement stairs. As Loren had promised, I had no direct contact with his family.

"Shouldn't I at least meet them?" I asked on day four. What if something happened while Loren was out—a leaking pipe or electrical mishap?

"You can meet them at the showcase next week," he said. "They're planning to be there."

"What showcase?" I asked. Evidently, he was talking to his family, just not in my presence. We didn't really know each other, I realized. We were more like playmates than friends. He was more serious on his home ground. I saw worry lines between his eyes a lot more than I saw his dimples.

I avoided leaving fingerprints on the table. Loren spent hours in the bathroom practicing his routine. As his voice rose and fell, I studied what could be seen through the long window near the ceiling on the south side of the basement: a cluster of white geraniums, a spider repairing her web, and pale, freckled calves walking out to the garage—his mother, I guessed. She wore navy blue leather clogs. I saw feet in scuffed green Doc Martens I presumed were Erica's.

My belongings were stowed in my suitcase and a small, dented box in the corner. I'd brought a few of the stones I'd gathered at the beach along with the modest purchases I'd made in Chicago—some toiletries, a few used paperbacks, pajamas, and an assortment of casual summer clothes.

On day five, we set up a card table and began assembling the edges of a jigsaw puzzle depicting a Greek fishing village. Out of the blue, Loren said, "I need to leave town for a while, maybe a couple of weeks." He told me that a friend of his on the East Coast needed some help. Friend? East Coast? Some help? Really—could he have been more vague?

Yet it would hardly have been fair to chide him. Whatever it was that we were to each other, we weren't confidants.

"That's okay, isn't it?" he asked, a slight edge to his voice.

"Sure," I said. "I'm just surprised, I guess."

What about the comedy showcase? What about me?

On the sixth day he called for an Uber and left. "I'm catching a train at 7:30," he said. "I'll call you soon."

Six days! I felt tricked. The barely started jigsaw puzzle taunted me.

I searched cupboards and drawers looking for clues—of what, I didn't know. Did I actually think Loren was part of some organization plot to lure me to Carbondale?

More likely, his old friend was an ex- or future-girlfriend—a more straightforward damsel in distress than me. Or maybe it took him only five days to remember why he'd left Carbondale in the first place or five days to realize he couldn't stay here with me.

I flipped through an old credit union calendar and studied matchbook covers but found no notes, cryptic or otherwise. I cringed when I knocked over a chair. I watched the bushes and trees in the backyard trying to decide if the leaves were thick enough to hide someone. I filled in a patch of bougainvillea on the puzzle.

Late afternoons I crept to the top stair and sat listening to the murmur of conversation and muffled clatter of cookware beyond the door. Nothing in the apartment below seemed to belong to Loren. No ukulele, no clothing, no books with his name in them.

Before leaving Chicago, I had withdrawn $1,000 in cash from the bank account and hid $100 bills amongst my meager belongings. A bill in a jeans pocket, in a rolled-up sock, in the pages of *The Murder at the Vicarage*.

At some point I would need to leave the apartment but not quite yet.

I scanned my body for irregularities and rashes. I palpated my breasts and fingered my cheekbones and eye sockets. I moved $100 bills from one book or pocket to another.

The weather stripping around the door to the outside was coming undone. I spent long stretches of time gawping at the doorknob, nearly certain someone was coming for me. Eventually, I'd force myself to eat something and talk myself down: *Stop being a crazy person—no one cares about you.* And then, at some point, I would resume my vigil.

I stared hard at the knob—brass, dull, and dinged. Then, a tickle in my nose. A prickly ball of heat surged up from my abdomen and settled in my throat.

The doorknob rattled. *Click-click-click* and a shiver of metal.

I held my breath waiting for the door to bang open, a fist to punch through the window.

I smelled burned hair. My mouth felt parched. I waited for at least a half hour, but nothing else happened.

Some hours later the idea came to me that no one had been outside the door—that I had been responsible for rattling the doorknob. Wouldn't that be an interesting development?

I snorted, thinking of Loren's comment about amnesia. Telekinesis was something that only happened in movies, right?

Audrey's departures and arrivals were marked by her diesel Rabbit rumbling beneath the carport at the side of the house.

I think this was a Wednesday. Five minutes after she'd returned from work, I heard a knock on the door at the top of the stairs. The door opened. "Hello?" a voice called down. "Margo?"

"I'm here." I was propped up in the foldout bed eating a cold-in-the-center Hot Pocket.

Audrey stepped down three steps, stopped short. "Do you know when Loren's getting back?" The rest of her body matched her shins. Her skin was densely freckled. Her strawberry blonde hair was pulled back in a ponytail. Her clothes were smooth and pale.

"Not exactly. He said maybe a couple of weeks." I tugged at the hem of my shorty pajama bottoms.

She surveyed the basement and sighed. "I couldn't remember what he told me."

"It didn't sound definite." Did she think it strange that I was still here, without him? What had he told her about me?

Audrey waved an envelope. "When you speak to him, would you please let him know that I'm going to have to charge you—him—for cable?"

"How much is it?"

"It's a matter of principle."

And/or she needed an excuse to meet the woman who was living in her basement. "I can pay you now, if you tell me how much we owe you," I said.

"I always told myself that if Dean dropped dead, the first thing I'd do was cancel the goddamn cable, and now he's as good as dead to me, but . . ."

"Who is Dean?"

She gave me a look—her eyes seemed to tighten. "How much did Loren tell you?"

It was hard to hold her gaze. "Not much," I admitted. "He told me you'd been through a rough patch."

"That's a good one," she said. "Dean is Loren's father. In any case, it's $79.99—what Dean has us signed up for. If you only want basic, it's $29.99."

She left before I could ask if a certain loud, intermittent buzzing belonged to the refrigerator, if I could use her washing machine and dryer, was the library within walking distance, had she recently cleaned with steel wool? I'd been smelling the rusty, soapy smell of used Brillo pads.

⟡

I couldn't remember how long it had been since I left the apartment. Had Loren already been gone for over a week? Alone again, I felt as flimsy as a paper doll. Surely this agoraphobic tendency was something new. I'd taken a job in Africa!

If I had been living in North Carolina before whatever happened happened, I probably would have put my things in storage. I would have told people that I might have difficulty staying in touch. Did this explain my lack of possessions and people?

I'd forgotten all about the cell phone. I almost missed Loren's call because it was at the bottom of my clothes box.

"What's new with you?" he asked, casual as can be.

"Your mom asked me about cable the other day. If you want it, we need to pay for it."

"No problem," he said.

I heard people talking in the background. I listened hard, wondering where he was exactly.

"Anyway, how are you doing?" he asked.

There was no good answer to that question. "Okay, I guess."

"What's wrong? Is Mom upset?"

Far from it. For the past two Thursdays, a man had joined Audrey for what sounded like ballroom dancing. I recognized the waltz, the tango, and maybe the cha-cha. The peppy music, the scrape and shuffle of their feet and frequent gales of laughter suggested a giddy kind of happiness.

"When are you coming back?" I asked.

"I'm not sure. Things are still up in the air."

I pictured Loren in a lime-green hot-air balloon floating somewhere over the Eastern Seaboard.

"People are counting on me, you know?" he added.

"If you say so."

"I think I still have a bike in the garage," he said. "An old Schwinn. Feel free to use it."

"What arrangements did you make with your mom? What am I supposed to do?"

"I've got to go," he said. "I'll call again soon."

"Loren—"

"Goodnight."

It was just a little past noon—1 p.m. Eastern time. The mistake didn't necessarily mean anything.

—

Happily, the hide-a-bed was tucked away and I was fully dressed when Audrey knocked on the door a few mornings later. It must've been a Saturday.

"I'm sorry if I was rude the other day," she said. "Would you like to come upstairs for a cup of coffee?"

The kitchen walls were a glossy yellow and new cabinets gleamed white, so the smell of fresh paint made sense. Sunlight pummeled us through the large windows and sliding door, none of which had blinds or curtains. A tag on the corner of the long oak table announced its sale price. Audrey scraped it off and pulled out a chair for me, pushing aside a stack of thick books. The coffee was very strong, and the light stung my eyes.

"Maybe you'll understand if I explain what happened with Dean," she said. Audrey's eyes were light green. (I suddenly couldn't quite picture Loren beyond his 70s rocker hair and loud shirts.)

Her eyebrows were drawn together as she told the story. Over the previous five years, her husband had embezzled a considerable sum of money from the financial investment firm that employed him. Dean's crime had been discovered and he was prosecuted. In June he'd begun a fourteen-month prison sentence.

I nodded—what could I say?—and marveled at the extent of Loren's understatement and omissions.

"The lawyers were able to prove that the house and cars had been paid off before he discovered his criminal tendencies, so at least we were able to hang on to that much," she said. "Anyway, we're moving on."

The kitchen had a wide doorway and a pass through to a dining or family room—its function ambiguous because the room was empty. I must have been staring.

"I'm starting from scratch upstairs," Audrey declared. "I don't need a single additional reminder of my marriage—not one chair, ottoman, or candlestick."

"The secret life of objects," I said without thinking—a scrap of something remembered.

"What?"

"Nothing," I said. "The kitchen is very cheerful," I blurted out before she could ask me a question.

"That's right," she said. "Cheer is exactly what I'm after."

I stared at the spines of the books Audrey had pushed aside: *An Invitation to Indian Cooking*, *The Africa Cookbook*, *Managerial Epidemiology*, and *Health Assessment in Nursing*.

"Loren told me you were taking classes . . ."

Audrey cleared her throat. "Right. It's part of my life makeover."

"I thought he said you were already a nurse, though."

"I'm an RN. I'm enrolled in a BSN program—bachelor of science in nursing with a minor in health care management."

"Are you liking it?"

"I haven't been a student for a long time and I'm taking two classes this summer, so it's tough. But yeah, it feels great to be moving forward."

"Do you mind if I ask you about the dancing?"

She grinned, revealing dimples I recognized as matching Loren's. His eyes were brown, I remembered, and he had a slight dent on the bridge of his nose.

"Not at all," she said. "I guess it would be hard to miss that."

She told me that one Saturday about a month ago, Dusty the mailman rang the doorbell and handed her a neatly wrapped loaf of banana bread along with the day's allotment of catalogs and bills.

"He'd baked it himself! He told me he'd heard what happened and was sure I deserved better than Dean. I invited him for dinner."

It turned out that they had both been looking into taking ballroom dancing lessons at the Y and they enrolled together in the very next session.

It felt good, sitting there listening to Audrey talk.

"We're the stars of our class," Audrey told me. "Dean's got nothing to say about any of it, and I have only one word for him—divorce."

I wondered if she really believed this or if she just wanted to believe this. I hoped her bravado was real.

The thermal carafe of coffee seemed bottomless. My body was twitchy from so much caffeine. Each time Audrey refilled our cups, she vigorously stirred three sugars into hers and set down the spoon less than a quarter inch from the edge of the table. The spoon was all wrong there—sticky and bent and perilous. The bowl of the spoon caught the sun and reflected light flashed off it. I tried to avert my eyes.

"Goodness—I have been blathering on," Audrey said.

Again, the spoon snagged my attention. It seemed to shudder as I blinked.

"Loren told us about your . . . problems," Audrey said. Her expression was gentle but appraising. I resisted the urge to pat the bones on my face.

"Are you okay?" she asked.

I was way too jittery to elaborate on my state of mind. "As well as can be expected," I said.

I was staring at the spoon—silver and shimmery—and my throat burned and my hand twitched and the spoon began to fall.

I must have closed my eyes. The spoon must have landed, though I didn't hear it.

Then Audrey was bending over to retrieve it. Her face was flushed when she sat up and returned the spoon to the table. "I've decided to cover my gray," she said, adjusting her ponytail.

The spoon looked normal and perfectly capable of making sound.

"I should get going," I said. I had mostly dismissed the notion of telekinesis, but it had happened again. (Or I had blacked out for a moment and knocked the spoon with my arm.)

I smelled burning leaves, heard a noise from the hall—a footstep— and sensed someone approaching. Panic flared in my chest.

What a relief when Audrey swiveled her head toward the hallway and hollered, "Erica Jean, stop eavesdropping!" To me she said, "Thank you for listening. I have a good feeling about you, Margo."

This seemed like a nice thing to say—not something a person would say when they were about to ask you to move out. Then I flushed, realizing she probably felt sorry for me.

I swung open the apartment door and flipped on the overhead light.

"Hello," the girl said. This had to be Erica. Who else would be sitting on the sofa wearing those clunky green boots nearly blackened with rain?

I was returning from my first foray out of the apartment—an unsatisfying and unsettling walk, the air full of drizzle and the sound of distant sirens. I counted cats—in windows, traipsing through bushes—and got to five before I spotted a dark sedan dubiously parked a block away, engine off, driver slouched, and sprinted back.

"Nice to meet you, Erica." The surprise of her presence had set my heart thudding.

Her mouth formed into a half-smirk. "Are you a witch?"

I glanced at the door at the top of the stairs.

"I know, it's rude of me to come down here uninvited," she said.

When I didn't reply, she cleared her throat.

"I was watching you and Mom the other day," she said. "I saw what you did with the spoon."

I felt a surge of adrenaline. I'd pushed that incident out of my mind, but I could still recall the spoon quavering, the silvery strands running through Audrey's hair, the heat in my throat. "I don't know what you think you saw, but I'm no witch."

"I didn't think so," she said smugly. She pulled one of Loren's white tube socks from beneath the couch. "You don't really know my brother. And you don't know squat about me and Mom." She sounded angry but I knew her anger wasn't about me.

"Right. I'm just a person who's staying in your basement," I said.

She frowned at the paperback on the cocktail table: *Crooked House*. With her thumbnail, she picked at something stuck in the tread of her boot. She dislodged a speckled gray pebble. She shook the pebble in her cupped hands as if it were a die. "I'm glad you understand."

I was pleased by a malice so obvious that I didn't have to second-guess it. I smiled at her.

"What's wrong with your chin?" she asked.

My hand flew to my chin. Erica's grin was diabolical. How did she know that I worried about the bones of my face dissolving and had nightmares in which my chin melted into a knob of flesh?

"Do you have a driver's license?" she asked.

"Yes."

"I thought maybe not, because of your condition." She leaped from the couch. "See ya!" she hollered, taking the stairs two at a time.

How long had she been down here before I got back? Were those her fingerprints on the table?

I removed two $100 bills from the pages of *Crooked House* and slipped them under the insole of my left sneaker.

Telekinesis telekinesis telekinesis. I repeated the word another dozen times—nonsense sounds.

Still, something had happened. Erica saw it.

Was this another antivenom side effect? Or perhaps it was a previously undiscovered gift, like a person sitting down at a piano for the first time and discovering they could flawlessly play "Für Elise."

That a nosy, teenaged girl thought she'd discovered my "powers" wasn't at all good. I'd have to be more careful. I'd have to bring this thing under control.

Researching telekinesis was like crossing an internet bog—so many places to get stuck. I could read about spiritualism and Swedenborg and spirit mediums or the story of botanist J. B. Rhine who abandoned his study of plant physiology after hearing a lecture by Sir Arthur Conan Doyle promoting psychic research. Dr. Rhine founded a parapsychology lab at Duke University and made a big splash in the 30s and 40s, but scientific interest appeared to be sporadic after that, and scientific attempts to validate phenomenon such as ESP and telekinesis were inconclusive and Rhine's findings were discredited.

What about my own career path? Had I been lured away from academia by the organization's reputation or an above-average benefits package or the opportunity to work in Africa? When I applied for the job, had I seen the irony in being a do-gooding white person abroad, following in my parent's noble footsteps?

I knew some of my questions might be answered by googling myself. I could see that people in my field sometimes maintained professional online profiles. But I couldn't quite go there yet. I'd rather remain ignorant for a while longer than google my name and find nothing—discover I'd been erased or that I'd never existed at all.

I put away the unfinished jigsaw puzzle. I would use the card table for my practice. I made an entry in a spiral notebook I'd found beneath some old phone books in the cupboard.

Thursday, 4:20 PM, unsharpened pencil, 2 inches from left edge of table. Empty stomach. Mood: leery.

I stared at the pencil until my eyes were dry and my forehead ached. I stared at the pencil like an idiot. (I chose a pencil because it was lighter than a spoon. It would be easier to move, right? But maybe I had an affinity for metal objects.) Stop overthinking! I told myself.

Just looking at the thing wasn't going to make anything happen. I needed to recreate the sensations I'd had with the doorknob and the teaspoon. It had something to do with my stomach and throat. I contracted my abdominal muscles and imagined my throat getting warm. I focused hard on the pencil, the green letters— Ticonderoga—and the pink eraser. I willed the pencil to roll forward.

I gasped. Had it quavered a bit?

Maybe, maybe not. Certainly not convincingly. Something about the way I was looking at the pencil was wrong.

The upstairs doorbell rang.

I didn't *need* to do anything. No matter who I was—houseguest? tenant? squatter?—a person at the door had nothing to do with me.

When the doorbell sounded again, I bolted up the stairs and opened the door.

A woman with a tight, affluent face was rummaging in her black Coach handbag. Her silver-white hair was close-cropped. Her hands were older than her face, age-spotted and swollen-knuckled.

"Is Audrey here?" she asked as she entered. "Or Erica?"

"I don't think they're back yet," I said.

The woman pulled out a handful of Glide floss containers. The blue of the plastic matched her velour warm-up suit. She looked around the empty foyer and living room for somewhere to put them. "Here," she said, handing them to me. I cradled them awkwardly against my chest.

"Criminy, my feet are tired." We looked at her impeccable white leather Keds. Again, she surveyed the furniture-free space as if she might have missed a chair the first time.

"You're the girlfriend," she said. "I'm Ruth. Dental hygienist and mother of the notorious white-collar criminal."

"My name is Margo," I said.

"I hear that Loren's done a runner."

"He had to—"

"Is he coming back?"

"I, uh—"

"How's Audrey holding up?" She fussed with her purse strap. Her French manicure was flawless.

"She's doing okay," I said. "Although—"

"You know, Audrey would never have left Dean if this hadn't happened, so I suppose it's one of those blessings in disguise."

An inherited trait, then—this one-sided conversational style. I must have smiled.

"You have an opinion on that?" Ruth demanded.

"I'm in the market for undisguised blessings," I said.

"Precisely!" she said. "It shouldn't be so goddamned hard."

I was pleased to have pleased her.

"Audrey's like a daughter to me," she said.

She stepped toward me, peering at my mouth. I tightened my lips and stepped back.

"When was the last time you had your teeth cleaned?" she asked.

"I'm not sure."

Ruth spun in place and sighed. "What in the hell is going on around here?"

—

Saturday, 10:05 AM, unsharpened pencil, two inches from left edge of table. Stomach: full; bacon, egg, and cheese Hot Pocket. Mood: skittish.

I pressed my hand to my belly and tried to conjure heat. I imagined a glowing red ball behind my navel but felt only soft flesh and gurgling. I loosened my jaw and relaxed my tongue, prompting an egg-flavored burp.

I stared at the pencil. The number 3191 was imprinted to the left of Dixon Ticonderoga. The number felt familiar. Was it part of an old phone number or address?

I stared at the 2 inside the green hexagon. Should I know what HB stood for?

I stared at the pencil until my vision blurred and there was no movement whatsoever.

—

I'd maintained my habit of counting cats as a means to distract myself from indistinct shapes lurking between houses and inside parked cars. The walk to the library took only ten minutes, but most days I spotted more than a dozen cats crouched in windowsills and sunbathing on sidewalks and porch steps. My record was eighteen.

With gorgeous weather outside, the library was nearly empty. A psychic miasma of ignored books and discarded scraps of paper wafted through the stacks.

I decided to look up Uri Geller, another topic I'd avoided. Geller, spoons, telekinesis—it was too obvious. Plenty of material existed, yet like so much of my research, it was questionable. I could feel myself wanting Geller's powers to be real. The debunkers were in the majority, but what about the findings of the CIA and the scientists who presented their results in *Nature*?

I clicked on a link to a video of Geller appearing on *The Tonight Show* in 1973. (My grandparents had loved Johnny Carson.) After welcoming Geller, Carson expressed skepticism, and his claim to keep an open mind rang hollow. The crew had arranged an array of objects on a low table. Minutes dragged on as Carson urged Geller to move his choice of item and Geller stalled, said he wasn't feeling it yet, and Carson called for a commercial break. This cycle repeated several times, tension mounting. I felt hot tears well up. I was furious with Carson for his sly questions and with Geller for not demonstrating what he could do. Finally, Geller said he would try something—identify which of twelve opaque containers held water. He enlisted another guest, Ricardo Montalbán, to help. Montalbán agreed, smiling and gracious and smug. Sweat gathered at my hairline as Geller gazed at the table. I paused the video, strangely afraid of what would happen next. I would watch it later, I decided. This wasn't the day for more unpleasantness.

The apartment smelled strongly of pickle juice. It reminded me of the German restaurant my grandparents used to take me to in Milwaukee. I loved their spaetzle and potato salad, and the cabinets were full of decorative beer steins and boot-shaped beer glasses. The memory might have calmed me, if Loren hadn't chosen that moment to call.

This time he jumped right into the conversation. "This is taking a lot longer than I thought it would," he said.

"Apparently," I said.

It was eerily quiet on Loren's end, as if he was standing in a chamber of silence. I believed that Loren had taken the 7:30 train the day he left—the Saluki to Chicago. From there he could easily have traveled to points east, as he'd suggested, or almost anywhere in the continental United States. It didn't really matter where he was, but my difficulty imagining him in a particular place was starting to make him seem more like an abstract idea than a person I had briefly lived with.

"Things don't always work out the way you think they will," Loren said.

"Do you think I don't know that?"

"I don't know what you know."

"Everyone over the age of twenty-five knows that!"

"Are you angry? I get that it's kind of awkward, me leaving . . ."

"I'm just frustrated."

"Okay. I get that. But I'm not seeing a clear path forward."

"Loren! What are you saying? Are you even planning to come back?" I asked, thinking of Ruth's question.

"I don't have a plan right now. I guess that's what I'm trying to say."

"Where does that leave me?"

"Where do you want to be? Aren't you happy in the apartment?"

That was his question? Was I *happy?*

⁓

I was drinking coffee and eating pizza rolls, my book splayed open on the picnic table nestled in a shady corner in the backyard. A six foot wooden fence stood stalwart behind me. From this angle, the house did not look like a place for anyone's fresh start. The white siding was dingy and mottled with green and a half-dozen shingles were missing from the roof. A dark-gray cat stood as still and tall as an Egyptian statue near the redbrick chimney.

"Hello?" Coming around the side of the house, Audrey spotted me and waved. She was still wearing the top she'd worn to work but had exchanged her scrub bottoms for a pair of cutoffs. "What is it?" she asked, catching me gawping at the spot on the roof where I thought I'd seen a cat—although the cat might have been (probably was) too large to be real.

"There are a lot of cats in your neighborhood."

"Are there?" she said, absently, picking up my book—*A Pocket Full of Rye.*

"Were you looking for me?" I asked.

The hair color shade she'd chosen to cover her gray was darker than her natural color. It flattened the red, exaggerating her pallor. It made me uneasy how different she looked.

"I wanted to ask you for a favor."

"Okay." Audrey hadn't mentioned Loren again. How long would it be until she asked me about my plans, suggested I move on?

"Erica said she paid you a visit the other day." Audrey sat down on the bench across from me and looked at me expectantly.

"That's right." I checked the roofline again—no cat.

"How did she seem?"

"Fine . . . ?"

"I worry about her. She's very angry with Dean. She was so happy when Loren moved back, and then he took off again so soon . . ."

It wasn't just the hair color that had changed. Audrey's top was wrinkled, and her shins were stubbly.

"That's a lot," I said. "Is there something I can do—I mean, the favor . . . ?"

"Erica turned sixteen in May. She had driver's ed in the spring. Dean was supposed to be the one to take her out to practice. Ruth, his mother, was taking her out, but she's gone AWOL."

"I'm sorry, I should have told you earlier—Ruth stopped by yesterday afternoon when you and Erica were out."

"Typical—we don't hear from her for a month and then she drops in when she knows I'll be at work."

This didn't sound quite right, but Audrey had returned to her original subject.

"I could take her . . ." She sighed and her posture wilted. "I can't say I don't have the time. I have time to dance, after all. But . . . You're going to think this sounds weird."

"I doubt it," I said.

"I have this phobia about driving with anyone else in the car. I mean, I can't stand being in a car with anyone else as a driver or a passenger. I panic."

"Oh." Was that weird? I mean, compared to what?

I was focusing on the wrong thing, so her request caught me off guard.

She yanked herself tall, correcting her slouch. "I was wondering if you'd be willing to go out with her. She's very eager to get her license and we have an extra car—Dean's car—that she could drive. But she needs more practice before she takes her test." Her expression radiated a mix of hope and desperation.

Finally, I realized where this was heading, and I wondered what my own features were doing. "How much more?"

"I'm not sure. She has enough practice hours to qualify, but she hasn't been out in over six weeks."

I had no idea when I'd last driven a car. I was almost certainly unqualified to accompany a volatile teenage driver.

"I know it's a lot to ask," she added. She bit her lip and looked like she was about to sag again.

"I can take her out," I said. Someday, I would find the gumption to talk to Audrey about the apartment. For now, at least, I could contribute to the household in this small way.

"Oh, thank you!" Audrey jumped up and leaned over the table, encircling my neck and shoulders in an awkward embrace.

I pictured a battered mailbox, a dented fender. I wanted to believe these were the worst possible outcomes.

Tuesday, 7:30 PM, a teaspoon, 3 inches from the left edge of the table. Stomach contents: 8 ounces of water and five saltine crackers. Mood: uneasy.

I was still convinced it involved my stomach and throat. I took slow, deep breaths. I contracted my abdominal muscles. I focused my attention on the circle in the spoon's bowl that held the reflection of the overhead light. I held my head still and imagined pressing my finger to that bright spot and gently sliding it to the left. I felt a promising tickle in my throat, but the spoon didn't budge.

I rotated it so the bowl pointed toward the edge of the table. I pictured the muscles at the back of my throat and imagined elongating them like I do when I'm trying to get rid of the hiccups. I focused on the shadow of the spoon this time.

Nothing—except I was wracked with five violent sneezes followed by a coughing fit that left my throat raw. The spoon was impervious.

On the way to the library a couple of days later, I spotted twenty-two cats. The computer I thought of as mine was available, and my favorite librarian signed me in for its use. I registered all this as a good omen, inspiring me to return to my old search terms, so I was only a little surprised when I got a partial hit on an online forum for NGOs, a post titled "Antivenom cover-up?" The message had been posted eighteen hours ago: I'm looking for people who were hired between 2008 and 2009 who have experienced visual and olfactory hallucinations. Memory loss, too.

There was a single response: You're not the only one.

Yes! Finally!

I looked around, hoping I hadn't made a strange sound.

At the next station, a young man was briskly typing, eyes glued on the screen.

My elation evaporated. The post meant nothing. It was just words on a screen posted by someone identified as Waterdoc.

Although maybe it wasn't a person at all. A quick search confirmed that something called AI chatbots did exist, which meant that it was possible the organization had created a bot to lure in people, find out who knew what.

I took a deep breath and clicked back on the tab.

The post and comment were gone! (Of course they were gone.)

Someone had removed it. Waterdoc, thinking better of their post?

The interface was clunky. I couldn't figure out how to search for Waterdoc. I couldn't remember the name of the commenter. (Some researcher I was.)

Something like static electricity sizzled across my skin. My shirt was damp. Was it my sweat that smelled like strawberries? I held my breath as I deleted my search history and logged off.

When I returned from the library, I was almost sure someone had been in the basement. My skin still prickled.

I spoke my name out loud, and I knew someone was listening. I began searching for hidden microphones. Would I even recognize an electronic bug if I saw one? You're being ridiculous, I told myself, then carried on frisking sofa and chair cushions, revisiting all the places I'd searched before.

There's no such thing as privacy. I remembered a low, authoritarian voice saying this. A professor in college? I could almost picture a dark-haired man wearing a red bow tie. Even if you use cash, even if you use a burner phone, there are cameras everywhere, he'd said.

No wonder the organization had left me my cell phone. It was something I would recognize as mine. Something they could use to track me. I should have dropped it in the trash at O'Hare. Instead, I'd obediently followed the path laid before me.

I glared at its shiny screen and dialed the number still labeled Home.

"Hello, Deborah. This is Margo."

"Hello."

"You remember me, right—your former tenant?"

"I remember you."

"Oh, okay. You sounded sort of—"

"I'm in the middle of something. What can I do for you?"

"I was wondering if anyone had come around looking for me."

"No." Had she answered too quickly?

"You're sure?"

"Yes, I'm sure. Are you in some sort of trouble? I don't want any trouble."

"Just one more question. What can you tell me about how I arranged to stay with you? I'm sorry, I know it's strange, but I'm having trouble remembering."

"Like I told you before, you made a reservation online and paid for your entire stay in advance."

"How did I pay?"

"All that's handled through VRBO, and I've never had a complaint."

"I don't have a complaint. I was just wondering . . ." As I watched the digital clock on the kitchen counter, the time changed from 3:48 to 3:49. Had the clock been there when Loren and I first arrived? Wasn't a digital clock one of the places a spycam could be hidden?

"Wondering what?" Deborah asked.

Anyone might be observing my meltdown remotely. *Hey there!* I waved like a maniac in the direction of the clock.

"Never mind," I said. "Thank you for your time." I hung up.

What did it really matter if someone was watching me—Loren, Erica, the organization, the CIA? I wasn't doing anything wrong.

I wasn't important.

I lay back on the couch and closed my eyes and wondered if the blue moths would ever reappear.

—⁕—

I was awakened by Dusty arriving for dance practice. After a few minutes of muffled conversation, the music began: a Viennese waltz. Dances of the world had been a theme in my third-grade class. I could hear Miss Marx's voice guiding us: step-step-*glide*, step-step-*glide*. I thought the sprightly tune might be by Strauss. The dancing upstairs sounded clumsy. I heard footfalls where they should have been gliding.

The music stopped and restarted. I jumped up. I poured myself a glass of juice. The glowing red numbers of the clock taunted me. I unplugged the clock. I picked it up and put it down; I picked it up and shook it. I pried off the clock face and separated the clock's innards from its molded plastic casing. I examined the tiny circuit board. I tugged at a circular bit of plastic that might have been part of a speaker, and it cracked off in my hand. Brilliant.

Hearing Dusty and Audrey move into the kitchen, I scooped up the disassembled clock pieces. Their voices sounded subdued. An off night, perhaps. Normal people had their ups and downs.

The clock was just a clock, almost certainly. I hid the pieces in the cupboard.

Why did I keep looking for proof, I wondered, and what was I looking for proof of, and how did I think that finding it would help me in any way?

This had to stop.

—•

Dean's car was a lime-green Dodge Viper with two thick black stripes on the hood. Much to my relief, Erica was a smooth, confident driver.

"It's so weird," Erica said, "Moving this big old thing with basically just one foot and one hand."

"That's two hands for you, miss," I said, mock-sternly. Erica's hostility had abated now that I was a means to an end.

We were already several miles from the house, the furthest I had been since I arrived, but I felt relatively calm. At least, that's what I was telling myself. Full of resolve, I barely checked for traffic cameras above the intersections.

I still walked to the library every day. Instead of doing research on the computers, I mostly stuck to reading magazines and checking out the bulletin boards. There were three of them, jammed with announcements for local events and classes and community services I studied as if they might hold clues regarding my future. (Reading tutor? Physician's assistant? Speaker of conversational Italian? Zumba enthusiast?)

I would have to do something.

"Personally, I think it's crazy that they let kids my age drive. I'm grateful, but still."

"Mmmm."

"What do you think of Carbondale anyway?" Erica asked.

"I haven't really seen enough to have an opinion."

"Loren showed you campus, though, right?"

"Nope."

She shook her head in apparent disbelief. "Are you from the Midwest originally?"

"Kind of."

"What does that mean?"

"I grew up in Milwaukee." I still didn't know why the organization had flown me to Chicago. I didn't know why Loren had brought me to Carbondale.

"Do you still have family there?" she asked.

"It's a good idea to not talk while you're driving."

A series of one-way streets thwarted Erica, and we made a few extra loops to get through the downtown area. Two-story redbrick buildings with faded awnings and shops named Shoes-N-Stuff, The Thrift Store, and Magickal Hippie gave it a dusty left-behind feel.

I thought I was keeping my eyes on the road, but I must have zoned out.

"Here we are," Erica announced, pulling up in front of a long, unpainted concrete building.

"Is this campus?"

"Yep. And what you see here is a wonderful example of brutalist architecture: Faner Hall."

"I would've guessed a prison."

"Ha!" Erica kept driving, pointing out various buildings. The architecture ranged from brutalist to boring to Tudor-Gothic, with some of what must have been the university's first buildings resembling castles.

"I guess it's a lot different than UNC," she said after a while.

"What?"

"You went to University of North Carolina Chapel Hill, right? You got a bachelor of science in public health and an MS in environmental science and engineering."

"Did you memorize my résumé?" I asked.

"Not intentionally," she said. "I just have a good memory. After college you interned with the Thirst Project and then you returned to UNC as an assistant professor and researcher for the Water Institute."

"That's enough." My heart rate ramped up. Not looking up myself on the internet had been a mistake.

"You don't look like an environmental scientist. No offense," she said.

"Seriously. Can we not talk while you're driving?"

She pulled over.

"What's wrong with you?" she asked.

How could I explain how panicked I felt at the thought that she might know more about me than I knew myself? And at the same time, I wished that she did know more—that someone could tell me if I'd enjoyed the work, if I'd been content.

She sighed dramatically. "I was just curious, you know. We've never met any of Loren's girlfriends."

"I'm not his girlfriend."

"You moved down here with him."

"And now he's gone, as you know."

She gave me a shrewd look. I could see all sorts of questions bubbling up behind her green eyes. Then she asked, "How does Mom seem to you?"

She must be studying interrogation techniques in her spare time. Chapter 2: Keeping Your Subject Off-Balance.

"She was happy that I agreed to go out driving with you," I said.

"True."

"And she told me she was glad to be back in school."

"I know that's what she says. And she did seem to be doing really, really well earlier this summer. She seems kind of down lately, though."

I'd thought the same thing, hadn't I?

"My dad is such a jerk," Erica said. Her voice trembled.

"You're a really good driver, you know that, right?" I said.

"Thanks."

—◦

I knocked at the door at the top of the stairs, balancing the laundry basket on my hip. I turned the knob and half-stumbled into the kitchen.

Audrey flinched and held up flour-covered hands. "Are you okay?"

"I'm so sorry." This was why I usually waited until the house was empty to use their washer and dryer.

"There's nothing to be sorry for." Audrey resumed kneading dough at the countertop. "I was hoping to talk to you."

"Oh. Should I . . . sit down?"

"Go ahead and start your load."

"Okay. It'll just take me a minute."

I twisted knobs and added detergent, wondering exactly what was on her agenda. I could've kicked myself for not asking about her plans for the apartment or offering to pay rent. Going out on a few drives with Erica didn't exactly balance the books.

"There's fresh coffee," Audrey said when I returned.

I hesitated, remembering my over-caffeinated performance during our previous coffee klatch.

"Or beer?" she offered.

"A beer would be good, thank you."

As she rummaged in the fridge, I opened *The Africa Cookbook.* Only because it was at the top of the stack of books on the table, of course. I nonchalantly flipped through the table of contents.

She cracked open two pilsners and set them on the table. I slid the book aside. Audrey's roots were coming in lighter and looked pinkish next to the darker, dyed hair.

"Here you go." Her smile was tired.

"How are your classes going?" I asked as she sat down.

"I'm down to one class," she said. "I dropped Managerial Epidemiology."

"Oh."

"I got a C– on my first case study, and that was a gift. I worked on that thing for such a long time, but I just can't wrap my head around all the jargon. I felt like I was drowning."

"I guess every class can't be a winner," I said.

"Unfortunately, that one is required for my minor."

"Is the other class better?"

"It's fine, I guess. It's kind of boring. The material is familiar because I've worked as a nurse for so long, but there's still a lot to memorize. I have to wonder if this is the right program for me."

"Maybe you'll feel different after the summer session is over."

"I don't really want to talk about school," Audrey said. She grabbed the other books and put them on the chair beside her, out of sight.

"I'm not sure that Loren is planning to come back," I blurted out.

"Interesting," she said. "But not surprising."

"How so?"

"Much like his father, Loren does exactly what he pleases. I wouldn't want to venture a guess regarding his plans."

She stood and headed back to the counter. She slapped the dough into a ball and dropped the ball into a bowl and set a towel over the bowl. She moved with a weary deliberateness. I could feel the heaviness in her arms, the tightness in her shoulders. She cleared the counter and began wiping it down. I wished she would sit down and rest while the dough rose. I didn't want her to be discouraged. I admired her so much—working, mothering, remodeling the house, dancing—getting on with things. And more than that, of course, I wanted her to prosper because I craved evidence that a person could remake their life.

"Erica said the driving practice went well," Audrey said.

"That's right. She's a very good driver."

"I figured. She's an extremely competent young woman. I can't help but worry about her, though."

"We're going to go out again tomorrow, I think." I was relieved that the conversation had veered away from Loren, but I felt a little guilty in letting pass the opportunity to talk about the apartment.

Audrey sat back down and took a few long swallows of beer. "I'm glad you're going to be spending time with Erica. She says her friends have been treating her differently since the news came out about Dean."

"That can't be easy." I couldn't remember what it felt like to be sixteen, but I did recall the perplexed reaction I'd gotten from other kids when I told them I lived with my grandparents and my parents were missionaries living in Peru.

Our beers were nearly empty.

"She's lonely," Audrey said softly.

I heard in her voice that she was lonely, too. I guessed that she didn't have an agenda. She just wanted to talk.

I was lonely. I had been a lonely child and I was certain that I had been lonely in my Before.

The buzzer signaling the end of the wash cycle startled me from reverie. Audrey reached out and squeezed my hand before I got up to put my load in the dryer.

The damp, floral scent of the wet clothing stirred memories of my grandparents, as it always did, and I missed them fiercely. I would have to review our conversation. I didn't want to read too much into it, although it seemed just possible that Audrey and Erica were glad I was there.

—◦—

The woman who took the clipboard barely glanced at it. Perhaps it was only in my mind that all the unanswered questions on the medical history form were a problem.

Who is your local doctor? When and for what reason were you last hospitalized? Do you suffer from anxiety concerning dental care?

I was only in for a teeth cleaning, after all. A patient canceled at the last minute, and Ruth claimed the spot for me.

"I can tell you're going through a hard time, dear," she'd said when I tried to refuse. "But that's no excuse for letting your gums go to blazes."

I couldn't disagree with that, and Erica offered to drive me, so here I was, stretched out on the dental chair.

Only faint wrinkles marked Ruth's forehead and the skin around her eyes was taut.

"Not bad, huh?" she said, leaning over to fasten my bib. "I'm sixty-seven, you know."

"You look great."

"I've had work done, of course. No one wants to look at a wrinkly old hag while they're having their teeth cleaned."

I pictured the stitch marks behind her ears and above her hairline. I imagined strangers peeking beneath my skin and shuddered.

"The irony is that I spent all that money thinking I was going to get at least ten or fifteen years of use from this face—" She lowered her voice. "And now I may be dying."

Abruptly, she tipped back the chair and I felt blood pool behind my eyeballs.

"I'm going to do at least one round of chemo. No sense being a dunce about it."

"You have cancer?" I asked, trying to catch up.

"Pancreatic."

"I'm sorry to hear that."

"I should have said chemotherapy combined with immuno-therapy. It's a new approach, they tell me."

"When do you start?"

"What I want most of all is to not be a burden on Audrey or Erica. They have enough to deal with right now." She lifted an implement from the tray. "Now open up," she instructed.

I was glad no answer could be expected of me as she scraped at the back of my front teeth.

"I want you to turn to the left and open just a bit wider."

I tried to close my ears to the sound of metal against enamel. I tried to count the individual hairs of Ruth's eyebrows. The fluorescent lights overhead flickered a message I couldn't decipher.

"Nearly done," Ruth said. "Just some polishing to go." She frowned.

"What's wrong?"

"People always want to blame the mother," Ruth said. "But I refuse to wonder if I did something wrong with Dean." She daubed paste onto the end of the polisher. "Now open again, please."

The distance between our faces was intimate. I closed my eyes as she ran the instrument over my teeth. I rinsed and spat and waited for Ruth to raise me to an upright position.

"I have a favor to ask of you," she said, leaning even closer.

How was it that I already knew I would say yes?

Thursday, 7:30 PM, a teaspoon, 2 inches from the left edge of the table. Stomach contents: empty. Mood: calmish.

I abandoned my previous notions about my throat and stomach. If something was going to happen, it was my brain that would make it so—some combination of what I thought and what I saw.

Upstairs, clothes were tumbling in the dryer. I listened to its soothing rumble and snick. I thought of the warmth of clothes fresh from the dryer, holding a warm T-shirt to my face and inhaling deeply.

Opening my eyes, I squinted slightly, blurring my vision.

I began to trace the exact curvature of the spoon bowl, the narrowness of the tip and neck, and the bend and taper of the handle. Again and again, I traced the spoon's contours, memorizing its arcs and angles.

My tongue grew hot. I closed my eyes and saw the edges of the spoon glowing blue, a blue like the center of a flame. It was the blue that directed the spoon's movement—the spoon's glide toward the table's edge.

It hit the floor—a tiny victory! I was very thirsty, and my mouth tasted of burnt grass.

When my cell phone rang, I was dusting a bookcase that held an old set of encyclopedias, pretending that I wasn't looking for a bug. I was surprised to see the caller was Loren.

"How's Carbondale treating you?" he asked.

Were we really still doing this—pretending that his life and mine overlapped?

"I can't complain," I said. "How are things with you?"

"Same." His words were distorted by rustling static. I heard muttering and distant shouts and the squeak of shoe leather. "Everything's really all right?"

I could have said that if he was *really* so concerned about his family, he should come home. But I didn't want him to return, didn't want him sitting beside me on the sofa bed watching TV, unpacking his belongings, disrupting the balance of women and objects.

"Margo?"

"It's not for me to say."

"What do you mean?" he asked.

"You should do what you need to do."

"I'm trying," he replied.

We had too much in common—rootlessness, melancholy—to be of help to each other.

". . . not the right place . . . right now." He was speaking again.

The static grew worse. I heard a loudspeaker in the background.

He was in transit, I concluded. He was disappearing.

⁓

"Where are you going?" Audrey asked, as Erica and I passed through the kitchen. She kicked off her work clogs, sending them flying across the room.

"Driving practice," Erica said.

The phone rang.

"Okay, be safe," Audrey told us as she picked up the phone. Something funny had happened to Audrey's voice when she spoke again. "Actually, I am busy," she said to whomever was on the line.

"Shit," Erica said under her breath.

"What is it?"

"C'mon," she said, tugging at my arm.

Backing the car out of the garage took all of Erica's attention. Once she was facing forward she said, "Dad is such a cockroach. He refuses to give up and die."

"That was your dad on the phone?"

"They changed his status at the prison, so now he gets to call more often."

"Do you talk to him?"

"Not if I can help it."

"Did you and your dad used to be close?"

"Yeah, but now I realize that everything he said and did was just a big load of crap. He makes me sick."

"What do you mean?"

"Last time we talked, he went on and on, telling me how there was still some money out here, and he'd try to get a hold of it so he could help me with college. Like he could buy me."

"But your mom still talks to him?"

"If she doesn't pick up, he just keeps trying. He thinks he can wear her down."

"How so?"

"You know—he wants her to forgive him, to wait for him, the usual bullshit."

I didn't like thinking of Audrey being harassed.

This was a Saturday morning, just after ten. Erica pulled into the strip mall and parked in front of our destination: Today's Wig Store. My joining Erica to help pick out a wig was Ruth's favor. Ruth didn't want us to tell Audrey about her cancer, hence the bogus practice session. "She doesn't need anything else on her plate," Ruth explained. And Erica did?

The store was all pink and chrome. Wigs hung from the wall like thick pelts. Blank-faced wig stands stood on every flat surface.

A very tall woman with jet-black hair approached us. "I'm Jeanine and I'm here to help you select a wig. Which one of you do I have the pleasure of serving today?"

"I'm looking," Ruth said. "I'll let you know if I need help."

Ruth stared at Jeanine until the woman backed up near the wall, then she pulled on a short, blond wig and considered herself in the mirror.

"You look *vivacious*," Erica said, reading from the wig's display marker. "And tasteful and stylish."

"I look like a blonde-gray hedgehog," Ruth replied.

"The monofilament top combined with the natural feel of real hair make the 'Flawless' wig the ultimate in realism," Erica continued.

"Okay, a realistic hedgehog," Ruth said. "Who are they trying to kid?"

"So, try another one, for Pete's sake. They've got hundreds to choose from."

Ruth didn't look like a hedgehog, but she didn't look like herself, and the smooth-haired salt-and-pepper wig did glisten like animal fur. My scalp prickled. The wigs gave off a smell like new tires. At least, I thought they did.

"I'm starting to think this was a mistake. A turban will be fine and about $500 cheaper," Ruth said. She stroked the silver-blonde real-hair wig she held in her hand as though it were a cat.

Erica grabbed the wig from Ruth's hands and handed her a cropped gray one. "These synthetic ones aren't bad. And it's not like your hair isn't going to grow back," Erica said. "You're not making a long-term investment."

"Ain't that the truth."

"Grandma!"

Another saleswoman joined the first, lurking at the back of the store. Their hair seemed unnaturally shiny. Were they required to wear wigs to work?

"Don't make eye contact," Ruth hissed. She slipped on another wig. This one was wavy and teased.

"That one's nice," Erica said.

Ruth scowled at her reflection. "I can't believe I spent so many years and so much money and pain on my appearance. I'm an old woman, period."

"Stop it!" Erica said.

"There's no fool like an old fool."

Big, pretty tears streamed down Erica's face.

"I'm sorry, sweetie. I'm just feeling a bit down." Ruth pulled a fuzzy piece of tissue from her purse and handed it to Erica.

My hands were cold. The tire smell was stronger. Back at the dentist's office, Ruth had made it sound like this would be fun.

I grabbed a chic, silver, shoulder-length wig from a stand. "What about this one?" I asked.

Ruth slipped it on. She ran her fingers through the strands and shook her head from side to side. She pinned on a smile. "It might be nice to have a little length."

"I like it," Erica said softly.

"We'll take this one," Ruth told the women.

It had been quiet upstairs all afternoon and then I heard the *thunk* of something heavy landing on the floor in the kitchen. Without thinking, I ran up the stairs to investigate and swung open the door.

"Is everything—"

"Everything's fine." Audrey was on her hands and knees, sweeping pieces of a broken ceramic bowl into a dustbin.

"If you don't want to go for the weekend, we could just stay one night," a man was saying. He had a tanned face and legs and arms, a neat blond ponytail, and a sturdy physique.

"It just seems pointless," Audrey said.

I was still standing in the doorway when Audrey got back to her feet. She sighed. "Margo, this is Dusty. Dusty this is Margo."

"Nice to meet you." He made a polite interval of eye contact before turning back to Audrey. "The *point* is to enjoy ourselves and get a change of scenery."

"We're never going to be good enough to compete." She emptied the dustpan into the garbage.

"C'mon, Aud. We've just started. Who knows where we'll be in six months or a year?" He took the dustpan and wrapped an arm around her.

"Exactly." She shrugged out of his embrace.

She looked at me. For some reason I was still standing there.

"What does that mean?" Dusty asked.

Erica barged into the kitchen. "What's going on?"

"Dusty is just figuring out that I'm not really a fun person," Audrey said.

"You're plenty fun!" Dusty said.

"You're fun, Mom."

Audrey shook her head. "In any case, I don't want to go."

"Okay, okay," Dusty said. "I'm sorry for pushing. You're right, there will be plenty of other opportunities for something like this."

"You're not listening," Audrey said.

"I am," he insisted.

"I don't understand," Erica said. "What are you guys talking about?"

Dusty spoke first. "We were talking about whether to go to Chicago over Thanksgiving break to see a ballroom dancing competition."

"I'm glad we took the class at the Y, it was fun, but the party's over," Audrey said.

Dusty's tanned face crumpled. "What are you saying? Did I do something wrong?"

"You loved the class," Erica said.

"I'm finished talking about this," Audrey said. "I'm going to heat up a bowl of soup and then study. I have a test in Health Assessment tomorrow for which I am utterly unprepared."

"I can heat the soup for you," Erica said.

"Please. Just go—all of you."

For the rest of the evening, I tried to process the scene I'd witnessed—a scene from which I should have excused myself.

I should have left the moment I realized that the noise I'd heard was only a bowl breaking, or just after Audrey introduced me to Dusty, and especially after she looked right at me, breaking me out of my stupor. I could claim genuine concern, but if I couldn't do anything to help, I was simply a voyeur (as demonstrated by my creeping up the stairs to listen by the door).

The upstairs had been mostly quiet for hours. I'd heard only the scrape of kitchen chair legs, water running, the poignant squeak of a highlighter on glossy paper.

Was the desire to apologize a legitimate reason for knocking on the door a few minutes after nine? What about my hope for an opportunity to deliver a salient pep talk? (Because obviously I was in a terrific position to dispense life advice!)

I tapped on the door and opened it a crack when I didn't get a response, then stepped in. One of Audrey's textbooks lay open, key words highlighted in yellow and pink and orange. Something about her neat highlighting and the different-colored markers made my eyes well with tears.

I flipped through the chapter she was on—"Collecting Subjective Data." Much of the material seemed common sense—don't assume an old person is sick, don't ask leading or biased questions. But I could see that it was potentially overwhelming: the Stanford Sleepiness Scale, a sample genogram of a family's health history, mnemonics for Pain Analysis and Symptom Analysis, and acronyms galore.

I heard a moan and wooden sort of creak that might have been the house settling. Then I heard singing and drumming, not from the back of the house but around me, as if I was at the center of a circle of people.

As the music's tempo increased, my heart began to beat faster and I felt my blood ticking at my temples and was overcome by fear that I was going to fuck this up, but I didn't know what *this* was.

I closed my eyes and rested my hands on the countertop. After a few deep breaths, the music and panic receded. When I opened my eyes, I saw that I was almost touching the African cookbook.

I opened it at random and landed on a recipe that felt familiar: *Gari Fotoi.*

The recipe appeared in the section on Ghana. The organization had a half-dozen or so projects in Ghana. Over nine thousand snake bite cases were reported there each year.

My pulse quickened and I thought how easily I could be sucked back into my existential mystery and those months spent looking for answers that didn't exist.

I read the ingredient list. Gari, onions, tomatoes, tomato paste, smoked mackerel. I felt the sting of the fresh chili pepper on my tongue, smelled the aroma of onions sizzling in palm oil. I felt the weight of a heavy skillet in my hand.

Why not just decide that I'd been to Africa? Why keep waiting for my life to make sense?

I closed my eyes again. My mouth watered in anticipation of the taste of the spicy stew.

A few days later, we arrived home from driving—Erica's first time on the freeway—just in time to help Audrey bring in some groceries.

"How'd it go?" Audrey asked after we unloaded everything in the kitchen.

"It was a little scary at first, but I did all right," Erica said.

"She's an ace at merging," I added.

"That's good." The top button of Audrey's navy-blue cardigan hung by a single thread. The pearly blue button swung slightly as she began unloading the grocery bags.

"I talked to Grandma," Erica said. "She wanted to know if there was a good night to come over for dinner this week."

Audrey slapped a package of celery hearts against her palm as if it was a baton and frowned at the messy piles of school notes and books on the kitchen table. Beside the piles was an ugly glass vase stuffed haphazardly with stubby pink and white carnations and long-stemmed red roses.

"What about Tuesday night?" Erica asked. "You'll be past the test and—"

"Tuesday's fine. It will be lovely to see Ruth." She handed me a package of paper towels and pointed to the cupboard behind me. "Will you join us for dinner, Margo?"

Audrey was saying pleasant things, but her voice was oddly flat.

"That'd be great."

"We'll finish putting away the groceries. You can go ahead and study," Erica said.

Audrey tried a smile. "You're becoming quite the nag, dear."

"I know how much school means to you."

"Do you? Because I sure don't." Audrey tapped the textbook. "This school thing is for the birds."

Erica's face flushed. "That's not true."

"My mistake was thinking anything could be different for me."

Erica's eyes met mine, and I felt we shared a sense of Audrey unraveling.

"What are you talking about?" Erica asked.

Audrey waved her arms over her head as if dispelling smoke. "I'm talking nonsense. Don't mind me." She lowered her arms, shoulders slumped, a woman defeated. "Why don't you two go for a drive or something?"

Erica opened her mouth to speak, but nothing came out. Neither of us was going to point out Audrey's mistake. Erica looked desperately around the room in search of something to say, some way to lighten the mood or distract Audrey.

Naturally, her eyes landed on the flowers, the thing that didn't belong. The vase was the green of overcooked spinach and it had a large bulbous base.

"Who are the flowers from, Mom? Dusty?"

"Yep—"

"That's great—" Erica started to say, perhaps, like me, hoping for a reconciliation.

"And Dean."

"Oh," Erica said softly. She tugged on a carnation.

"I just stuck both bouquets in there together," Audrey explained. "I couldn't quite bring myself to throw them away."

When Ruth came over on Tuesday, she descended the stairs and circled the basement like a building inspector. "I just couldn't quite picture it," she said. "You living down here." She shook her head as if she had water in her ears. The wig swung elegantly.

I remembered the way Ruth had thrust the dental floss containers at me.

The first time I'd seen Erica, she'd been holding a pair of wet, green shoes in her lap.

I remembered Audrey's thin wrist as she poured me cup after cup of coffee. The shimmer of wigs in the store. The day I'd seen only two cats. The pulpy, sweaty smell of the library.

I had real memories now. Every day I was collecting them—shared experiences, verifiable events—a store of memories to draw on.

"Why are you wearing the wig? You haven't started to lose your hair yet," Erica asked.

"I want to get used to how it feels. I have to say I'm very glad we went with the more expensive one. It isn't nearly as hot as I thought it would be."

"What a ringing endorsement," Erica said.

"I like my wig. It's lovely. It's just the thing."

"You're just saying that."

"I'm not just saying that. What happened last week was simply a small lapse. You can understand that, can't you?"

"Okay, okay," Erica said.

Erica told Ruth about the flowers.

"Men are so unoriginal," Ruth said.

Upstairs, the phone rang. We heard Audrey's hello. A significant pause.

"Dad." Erica groaned.

We edged closer to the stairs. Erica and I stepped carefully onto the first step, then the second, Ruth one step behind us, a stealthy trio, making our way to the top.

Audrey was speaking. "You don't need to concern yourself with anything except taking care of yourself."

"He's telling her that he's putting out feelers," Erica whispered, "how he's going to be able to help out financially as soon as he's released."

"I'm doing just fine on my own," Audrey said, but she inserted nothing in the space where she might have presented the evidence.

"He's telling her that he's so sorry to have put her through this ordeal and he'll do whatever it takes to make it up to her," Erica said.

"I'm not mad at you, not really," Audrey said.

"He's telling her that once he's released he'll take her on a trip somewhere."

"I wanted to go to Paris ten years ago, Dean." Audrey was still pushing back, but the fight was leaking out of her voice.

I listened hard. The silence told us she was listening to Dean. I guessed she was leaning against the counter. I bent over to look under the crack beneath the door. Yes, that's where she was. That meant the flowers were on the table just across from her.

Ruth and Erica tensed beside me, barely restraining themselves from bursting into the kitchen. Audrey's resolve was weakening, but surely that was only temporary. This was just a bad couple of weeks. She just needed to get off the phone before she gave anything up.

I closed my eyes, inscribing in my mind that odd, thick bulge at the bottom of the vase. My throat tickled and I swallowed hard. I had to be able to do this. I had to be able to do something.

I sensed Ruth and Erica both holding their breath beside me, anticipating the next moment.

I only needed two centimeters, if that.

Then—I gasped and Audrey squealed and the vase cracked against the floor like a rock splitting. My throat was so dry.

Ruth gathered Erica and me into her arms for a quick Chanel No. 5-laced squeeze. Then she knocked loudly on the door and slid past me.

"Surprise!" she said. "Hello dear."

Audrey stood with her mouth open. She looked from the phone in her hand to the broken vase to her mother-in-law. The water from the vase had already spread into a large puddle.

"Now close your mouth and put some water on. We've come for tea," Ruth said.

Erica plucked the phone from her mother's hand and returned it to its base. Audrey moved toward the stove with a zombie stutter step. "What's . . . ?" Her voice trailed off.

"Margo," Ruth told me. "Don't just stand there. Get out the cups and saucers."

Erica grabbed a dish towel and began swabbing at the pool of water. The vase had simply cracked in two, and I picked up the pieces and set them on the counter.

"I'm just going to throw these flowers away," Erica said firmly.

"Audrey," Ruth said. "Turn the water on."

"Okay, then," Audrey said, snapping out of her trance and twisting the dial on the stove.

Okay, then. A broken vase, an interrupted phone call, a kitchen full of women, this hiss of tea kettle. It was a start.

⁓

About the Author

Valerie Vogrin's collection *Things We'll Need for the Coming Difficulties* was awarded the Spokane Prize for Short Fiction (Willow Springs Press, 2020). She is the author of the novel *Shebang*, and her short stories have appeared in journals such as *Ploughshares*, *AGNI*, *Hobart*, *Memorious*, *Zone 3*, and *The Los Angeles Review* as well as in *2011 Pushcart Prize XXXV: Best of the Small Presses*, *The Best Small Fictions 2015*, and *New Stories from the Midwest 2020*. Her work has been supported by residencies at the Virginia Center for the Creative Arts and the Anderson Center for Interdisciplinary Studies. Valerie received her MFA from the University of Alabama. She's a professor of creative writing at Southern Illinois University Edwardsville. She lives with her husband, dog, and cat on a tiny unnamed lake in Moro, Illinois.

About the Book

Expedition is set in Adobe Garamond Pro digital fonts created by Robert Slimbach from the Adobe Originals program and based on orginal metal types by Claude Garamond and Robert Granjon that were designed and cast in Paris, France in the sixteenth century. This book is also set in Montserrat digital fonts designed by Julieta Ulanovsky in 2011 and inspired by the early twentieth century Buenos Aires neighborhood, Montserrat. The cover features artwork by Sophia Lavallee. The spoon vector ornament used throughout the cover and book was created by Graphic&Illustration through Adobe Stock. The cover and book were both designed and typeset by Jay Aja at the University of Tampa Press.